BAMBI'S FIRST DAY

By Felix Salten *& Illustrated by* Gijsbert van Frankenhuyzen

He came into the world in the middle of the thicket, in one of those little, hidden forest glades which seem to be entirely open but are really screened in on all sides.

There was very little room in it, scarcely enough for him and his mother.

He stood there, swaying unsteadily on his thin legs
and staring vaguely in front of him with clouded
eyes which saw nothing. He hung his head, trembled
a great deal, and was still completely stunned.

"What a beautiful child," cried the magpie.

She had flown past, attracted by the deep groans the mother uttered in her labor. The magpie perched on a neighboring branch.

"What a beautiful child," she kept repeating.

Receiving no answer, she went on talkatively, "How amazing to think that he should be able to get right up and walk! How interesting! I've never seen the like of it before in all my born days.

Of course, I'm still young, only a year out of the nest you might say. But I think it's wonderful. A child like that, hardly a minute in this world, and beginning to walk already! I call that remarkable. Really, I find that everything you deer do is remarkable. Can he run too?"

"Of course," replied the mother softly. "But you must pardon me if I don't talk with you now. I have so much to do, and I still feel a little faint."

"Don't put yourself out on my account," said the magpie. "I have very little time myself. But you don't see a sight like this every day.

Think what a care and bother such things mean to us. The children can't stir once they are out of the egg but lie helpless in the nest and require an attention, an attention, I repeat, of which you simply can't have any comprehension.

They are helpless if you are not with them. Isn't it the truth? And how long it is before they can move, how long it is before they get their feathers and look like anything at all."

"Pardon," replied the mother,
"I wasn't listening."

The magpie flew off. "A stupid soul," she thought to herself, "very nice, but stupid."

The mother scarcely noticed that she was gone. She continued zealously washing her newly-born. She washed him with her tongue, fondling and caressing his body in a sort of warm massage.

The slight thing staggered a little. Under the strokes of her tongue, which softly touched him here and there, he drew himself together and stood still.

His little red coat, that was still somewhat tousled, bore fine white spots, and on his vague baby face there was still a deep, sleepy expression.

Round about grew hazel bushes, dogwoods, blackthorns, and young elders. Tall maples, beeches, and oaks wove a green roof over the thicket and from the firm, dark-brown earth sprang fern fronds, wood vetch, and sage.

Through the thick foliage, the early sunlight filtered in a golden web.

The whole forest resounded with myriad voices,
was penetrated by them in a joyous agitation.

The wood thrush rejoiced incessantly, the doves
cooed without stopping, the blackbirds whistled,
finches warbled, the titmice chirped.

Through the midst of these songs the jay flew,
uttering its quarrelsome cry, the magpie mocked
them, and the pheasants cackled loud and high.

At times the shrill exulting of a woodpecker
rose above all the other voices.

The little fawn understood not one of the many songs and calls, not a word of the conversation. He did not even listen to them. Nor did he heed any of the odors which blew through the woods.

He heard only the soft licking against his coat that washed him and warmed him and kissed him.

And he smelled nothing but his mother's body near him.

She smelled good to him and, snuggling closer to her, he hunted eagerly around and found nourishment for his life.

While he suckled, the mother continued to caress her little one. "Bambi," she whispered.

Every little while she raised her head and, listening, snuffed the wind. Then she kissed her fawn again, reassured and happy.

"Bambi," she repeated. "My little Bambi."

TO BENJAMIN POTTER

Gijsbert

Illustration Copyright © 2008 Gijsbert van Frankenhuyzen

Sleeping Bear Press®

310 North Main Street, Suite 300
Chelsea, MI 48118
www.sleepingbearpress.com

© 2008 Sleeping Bear Press is an imprint of Gale, a part of Cengage Learning.

Printed and bound in China.

First Edition

10 9 8 7 6 5 4 3 2 1

Library of Congress Cataloging-in-Publication Data

Salten, Felix, 1869-1945.
Bambi's first day / from the original story written by Felix Salten ;
illustrated by Gijsbert van Frankenhuyzen.
p. cm. — (Classic stories from Sleeping Bear Press)
Previously published as the first chapter of: Bambi.
New York : Simon & Schuster, 1928.
Summary: A fawn spends its first moments of life in
a forest glen, safely sheltered by its mother.
ISBN 978-1-58536-422-0
1. Deer—Juvenile fiction. [1. Deer—Fiction. 2.
Animals—Infancy—Fiction.] I. Frankenhuyzen, Gijsbert van, ill.
II. Salten, Felix, 1869-1945. Bambi. III. Title.

PZ10.3.S176Bar 2008
[E]—dc22   2007046316